GERONIMO
STILTON

Published by Sweet Cherry Publishing Limited
Unit 36, Vulcan House,
Vulcan Road,
Leicester, LE5 3EF,
United Kingdom

First published in the UK in 2018
2018 edition

ISBN: 978-1-78226-369-2

Text by Geronimo Stilton
Art Director: Iacopo Bruno
Graphic Designer: Laura Dal Maso / theWorldofDOT
Original cover illustration by Roberto Ronchi and Alessandro Muscillo
Concept of illustration by Gògo Gó, produced by Danilo Barozzi, Silvia Bigolin, Francesco Castelli
and Christian Aliprandi with assistance from Lara Martinelli
Initial and final page illustrations by Roberto Ronchi and Ennio Bufi MAD5, Studio Parlapà and
Andrea Cavallini. Map illustrations by Andrea Da Rold and Andrea Cavallini.
Cover layout and typography by Elena Distefano
Interior layout and typography by Rhiannon Izard and Amy Wong
Graphics by Michela Battaglin and Yuko Egusa
© 2006 Edizioni Piemme S.p.A., Palazzo Mondadori – Via Mondadori, 1 – 20090 Segrate
© 2018 English edition, Sweet Cherry Publishing
International Rights © Atlantyca S.p.A. – Via Leopardi 8, 20123 Milano, Italy
Translation © 2006, Edizioni Piemme S.p.A.

Original title: *Il mistero degli elfi*
Based on an original idea by Elisabetta Dami

www.geronimostilton.com/uk

www.sweetcherrypublishing.com

Printed and bound in Turkey

Geronimo Stilton

THE CHRISTMAS TOY FACTORY

Sweet Cherry
Publishing

TWO BLOCKS OF ICE

It was a cold – I mean, **FREEZING** – I mean, teeth-chattering December morning. Snow covered New Mouse City, and I was trudging through it on my way to work. **Brrr!** My paws felt like two blocks of ice.

I finally got to the office and ... Oops, silly me! I forgot to introduce myself. My name is Stilton, *Geronimo Stilton*. I am the publisher of The Rodent's Gazette, the most famouse newspaper on Mouse Island.

As I was saying, I got to the office and sat down at my desk. But before I could start working, a plump, furry mouse burst through the door. It was my grandfather William Shortpaws, also known as **Cheap Mouse Willy**. Rats!

Don't get me wrong, I love my grandfather. But for the past month, he has been driving me up a clock!

Grandfather is the founder of The Rodent's Gazette. He started it a long, long time ago. He doesn't work here anymore. Lately, he's been into golf. But he still loves to stop by the office and check up on things.

Grandfather is one tough, no-nonsense rodent. His favourite

10

saying is: ALL WORK AND NO PLAY MAKES A MOUSE RICH, RICH, RICH!

Before I could even squeak, "Hello," Grandfather William began thumping his paw on my messy desk. A stack of papers crashed to the floor. "Grandson, this desk is a **DISGRACE!** Have you been working or eating cheese bonbons? Remember, I built this company with my own bare paws. If you're not careful, I'm going to come back and you'll only be in charge of the water cooler!" he thundered, pulling my whiskers.

I gulped. My worst nightmare is my grandfather coming back to head The Rodent's Gazette. And lately, I was afraid he might do just that!

"I'm doing my best," I squeaked meekly.

Grandfather rolled his eyes. "Tell it to the paw!" He smirked, holding one paw towards me. Then he pulled my whiskers again. And stormed out.

I got right to work. What else could I do? I was worried. **And besides, I don't know a thing about water coolers.**

I DREAMED I WAS SLEEPING

It snowed every day for a whole week. I had to put snowshoes on my paws just to get to work! I would have loved to call in sick, but I couldn't. What if Grandfather William found out? I'd be out of a job faster than you could say *'egg and cheese on a cream cheese bagel'*. Instead, I got up every day at the crack of dawn and dragged myself to the office. There I read manuscripts, signed cheques, and researched stories. **I was so busy I never even took a lunch break.** I just nibbled on some stale Cheddar crackers that I kept in a bowl on my desk.

Finally, at midnight, I'd head home. I was so tired I'd fall into my bed and start snoring before my snout even hit the pillow. I dreamed I was sleeping.

The days flew by. I was **EXHAUSTED**! But I had to keep working. I couldn't let Grandfather William take over the newspaper. I loved my job. **Too bad it was taking over my life!**

UNCLE GERONIMO, WHY DIDN'T YOU COME?

On the morning of December 24, something awful happened. I was at my office reading some mail that had piled up on my desk. I came across a letter from my dear, sweet nephew Benjamin. When I read it, I nearly jumped out of my fur. It was an invitation to his Christmas play. I twisted my tail up in a knot.

"December 24!" I squeaked. **"Mouldy mozzarella balls, that's today!"** I was so busy with work that I had completely forgotten.

dear Uncle Geronimo,
Can you please, please, please come to my school's Christmas play on december 24 at 9 a.m.?
Can't wait to see you!
love,
benjamin

I ran to Benjamin's school as fast as my paws could carry me. But it was no use. When I got there, the play was already over.

Principal Sharp Whiskers shook his head when he saw me. "Mr. Stilton, why are you so late? Your nephew is **CRUSHED**," he scolded.

Just then, I noticed a little mouse sitting all alone on the stage. It was Benjamin. He looked at me sadly.

"Uncle Geronimo, why didn't you come? You always come to my Christmas play. And this year I had the best part. I was one of the fur trees," he said.

I felt awful. How could I have let my favourite nephew down? I grabbed his paw. "Come on, I'm going to buy you an early Christmas present," I said, smiling.

I took him to the best toy store in town, the Rollicking Rodent. Have you ever been there? The place is huge! The salesmouse showed us a SUPER-SCARY CAT MASK and a squeak-controlled race car. But all Benjamin wanted was to go home. When we got there, he ran inside before I could even say goodbye.

I felt lower than a sewer rat. I hung my head and headed back to the office.

What else could I do? I had so much work to do!

I Don't Have Time for Surprises!

When I got back to the office, I slumped behind my desk. **What a rotten day.** How could I have forgotten my favourite nephew? If only I didn't have so much work to do. Just then, I noticed the light on my answering machine blinking. I hit the message button. "Why aren't you at your desk, Geronimo?! **DON'T MAKE ME COME IN THERE!**" Grandfather William's voice bellowed through the speaker.

I cringed. Suddenly, I heard a knock at the door. Who could it be? A delivery mouse wheeled in a huge package. It was decorated with a shiny bow and some tiny yellow bananas.

"I love bananas! B-a-n-a-n-a-s!"

I looked around to see who had spoken, but didn't see anyone.

Then, a sooty grey rat sprang out from the package. He was wearing a long trench coat and matching hat.

It was my friend Hercule Poirat, the famouse detective!

He handed me a little package. "Surprised, Stilton? I wanted to wish you a merry Christmas!" he shouted.

Before I could respond, I heard a knock at the window.

My eyes nearly popped out of my fur. A rodent was hanging in front of the window ledge. He had a crew cut and big, bulging muscles. He was dangling from a bungee cord.

I opened the window with shaking paws. Was he some kind of spy? Was he from another planet?

"Hey, fellow camper!" the rodent yelled. "Just dropping by to say happy holidays!"

It was my friend Burt Burlyrat,

otherwise known as B.B. We'd met at a survival boot camp deep in the jungle. Why would a scaredy-mouse like me go to boot camp? Well, that's another story.

Now my teeth began to chatter watching B.B. sway in the wind. **I felt like I was about to have a nervous breakdown.** Of course, Burt didn't seem to mind that he was dangling forty feet in the air by a little cord. Instead he just smiled at me and handed me a gift-wrapped package.

I was still worrying about B.B. when the door to my office slammed open again.

"Merry Christmas to you, dear Geronimo!" a magnificent voice sang out.

A beautiful rat wearing a scrumptious Cheddar perfume stood in the doorway holding a gift. She had amber-coloured fur, twinkling eyes, and a dazzling smile. It was my dear friend Squeaky Star.

Do you know Squeaky? She is

a very famouse singer. Her CD, *Under a Cheddar Moon*, has been number one on the charts for almost a whole year. We met a while ago on top of Kilimanjaro during another one of my crazy adventures. I'll have to tell you about it sometime.

"I see you already have guests," Squeaky said, smiling. "Why don't we all go out for a holiday lunch and you can open your Christmas gifts?"

CHEESE NIBLETS! I hated to be a Scrooge. But what could I say? I had so much work to do! And what if Grandfather William decided to stop by? He'd have my tail!

"Thanks," I said. "But I don't have time. You'll all have to go without me. I am too busy."

Disappointed, my friends headed out the door. Well, except for B.B. He lowered himself down to the pavement, instead. I tried to wave goodbye, but he never looked up.

I felt like the worst friend in the whole world.

I Don't Have Time to Travel!

The snow kept falling, thicker and thicker.

I had my snout buried deep in a pile of papers when my friend Petunia Pretty Paws stopped by. She is a fascinating mouse. I guess you could say I have had a **huge crush** on her forever. Too bad whenever I'm around her, I turn into a babbling, blundering fool. I stammer. I stutter. Sometimes I can't even tell my left paw from my right.

Petunia hugged me. "Geronimo!" she squeaked.

"Yes, um, that's me, Seronimo Gilton. I mean Geronimo Stilton," I mumbled, grinning.

Petunia giggled and grabbed my paw. "I have the most exciting news! I'm headed off to Australia after Christmas to film a documentary about dolphins. Why don't you come with me?" she squeaked. "Just think,

right now the sun is shining in Australia."

I stared out the window. Oh, it would be so nice to get away. Then I looked at the stack of papers on my desk.

"Ahem, thanks, but I'm really too busy to go," I said.

Petunia put her paws on her hips. "Yes, yes. I know you're a very busy mouse, but there are some things in

life that are more important than work, G," she scolded.

I chewed my whiskers. Maybe she was right. Maybe I should take a break. I was just about to say yes to Petunia when I noticed the big, framed picture of Grandfather William on the wall.

His piercing black eyes seemed to be glaring at me. ALL WORK AND NO PLAY MAKES A MOUSE RICH, RICH, RICH! Grandfather's voice echoed in my head. "Get working, Nephew!"

"Sorry, Petunia," I muttered as she turned and walked out.

I Don't Have Time to Celebrate!

After Petunia left, I tried concentrating on my work. I didn't even look out at the falling snow. I was interrupted by the sound of rodents **giggling** outside my door.

Suddenly, the door burst open. It was all of my co-workers.

"Merry Christmas to you, Merry Christmas to you, Merry Christmas, dear Geronimo!" they squeaked at the top of their lungs.

I was feeling grumpier and grumpier. How was I supposed to get any work done?

Before I had a chance to complain, Shorty Tao grabbed my paw. She dragged me away from my desk. "Want to help us decorate the Christmas tree?" she asked.

"How about a little cheesecake?" Ratsy suggested.

"Or a cup of hot Cheddar?" Patty added.

"Or you could help me hang up the mistletoe," Gigi said, winking.

I was beginning to get a rat-sized headache. I didn't have time for Christmas this year. I had too much work to do!

Right then, everyone broke into an ear-piercing chorus of 'Jingle Bells'. Now even my fur had a pounding headache.

Finally, I couldn't take it anymore.

"Enoooooooough!" I shrieked.

29

MOUSEANNA

A deep silence fell over the room. Everyone stared at me, stunned.

"Ahem, I just want everyone to, um, go back to work," I muttered.

Puzzled, Mouseanna waved a photo under my nose. It was a picture of the Christmas party we had last year.

"But, last year, you said you wished we could have a Christmas party every day!" she squeaked.

Last year's party!

I coughed and thought of Grandfather William. "Yes, well, I changed my mind," I mumbled as I slunk back to my office.

I felt awful. But I had a ton of work to do.

I sat at my desk and started to read a manuscript. Outside, it was quiet. In fact, the whole place was quieter than the **Whispering Whiskers Cemetery**. A horrible thought occurred to me: what if my co-workers were so mad that they were waiting behind my office door? When I opened it, they'd throw mouldy mozzarella balls at me!

I peeked out of the door. Everyone was seated at their desks, working silently.

I felt much better. Well, not that much better. Everyone did look kind of sad. **But at least I wasn't going to get hit with rotten cheese.**

I Don't Have Time for Christmas!

It was getting later and later and snowier and snowier.

I was still up to my snout in work!

Just then, my cousin Trap called.

"Hey, Gerry Berry, what are you still doing in the office? Get your tail out here! We're all waiting for you at the family's Christmas Eve dinner!" he yelled.

I shook my head. For some reason, I couldn't think of anything but work, work, work.

"I don't have time for dinners. I don't have time for Christmas. I'm just too busy," I muttered, thinking of Grandfather William taking over the paper.

My sister Thea grabbed the phone. "Geronimo, don't give me any of your

34

lame excuses!" she ordered.

Aunt Sweetfur got on the phone next. "My dear nephew, Christmas won't be the same without you!" she said, sighing.

But I had already made up my mind. **I had to finish my work, no matter what!**

DING, DONG

The snowy night went on. I worked and worked and worked until I heard the town's clock strike midnight.

**DING DONG DING DONG
DING DONG DING DONG
DING DONG DING DONG**

I was tired. So very tired. I wanted to go home and snuggle up in my bed. But it was like there was a little workaholic mouse inside my head. I knew if I stopped I would never finish anything!

Hours later, I finally finished. Now the only thing left for me to do was to write a story on the real spirit of Christmas to be published in the newspaper the next day.

To get some inspiration, I leafed through a book titled *The Story of Santa Claus*. But I was so tired that I fell asleep with my snout right in the middle of the book. **Snore, snore, snore ...**

The Story of Santa Claus!

According to ancient legend, Santa Claus lives in Rovaniemi, Finland. His house, however, is located in a secret and very isolated place called Korvatunturi. In Finnish, Korvatunturi means 'Ear Mountain' because it's shaped like two big bunny ears. It's from there that Santa can hear everything that all the children in the world say. That's how he decides which children deserve his gifts!

The elves are Santa's helpers. They make the gifts that he distributes from his famous sleigh, pulled by his nine faithful reindeer. Here they are! Each reindeer has its own name and personality.

Dasher

Captain of the
reindeer team

Rudolph

The red-nosed
reindeer

Donner

Believes she should be
captain of the reindeer team

Comet

Once flew so high, he almost
collided with a comet!

Blitzen

His antlers always
point north!

Dancer

Is Prancer's
twin sister

Prancer

Like her twin,
loves to dance

Vixen

Is the most graceful
and acrobatic of all
the reindeer

Cupid

Has been married to
Vixen for more than
two hundred years

KNOCK! KNOCK!

I don't know how long I had been sleeping, but I woke up mid-snore. There was somebody knocking at my window. **Knock, knock!** A weird little face was

squashed against the windowpane.

"**MOULDY MOZZARELLA!**" I squeaked. I was so frightened all of my fur stood at attention.

A shrill little voice yelled back, "Hey there, open up. I've got something to tell you!"

My teeth began chattering so hard I probably had permanent tooth damage. I'd never be able to eat hard cheese again. No more super-mature Cheddar. No more Swiss.

I was still thinking about hard cheeses when a chubby elf with a tiny beard tumbled in through the fireplace. **MOULDY MOZZARELLA!** That's what I get for not opening the window, I guess.

"Are you the magazine mouse?" he asked, looking me up and down suspiciously.

I blinked. "Well, actually, I run a newspaper," I said. "My name is Stilton, *Geronimo Stilton*."

"Yeah, yeah, same thing," the elf muttered.

He told me his name was Ding-Dong. Santa Claus had sent him to find me. "He wants you to come and visit," the elf explained.

I was shocked. Why would Santa Claus want to see me? Ding-Dong didn't know, either.

But how could I say no to Santa?

I'm Too Young to Die!

The next thing I knew, I was sitting in the back of a sleigh pulled by nine prancing reindeer.

"Hit it, guys!" Ding-Dong shouted. Instantly, the reindeer took off into the sky!

 Up, up, up we flew. Clouds swirled around us. I held on for dear life. **Did I mention I'm afraid of flying?**

Meanwhile, Ding-Dong was humming happily beside me. "Hey, Magazine Mouse, isn't this sleigh **awesome?**" he shrieked, zipping through the sky. Then, before I could squeak, **"No! Stop! I'm too young to die!"** he started showing me all of the flying tricks he could do. The sleigh dipped and soared up and down through the sky.

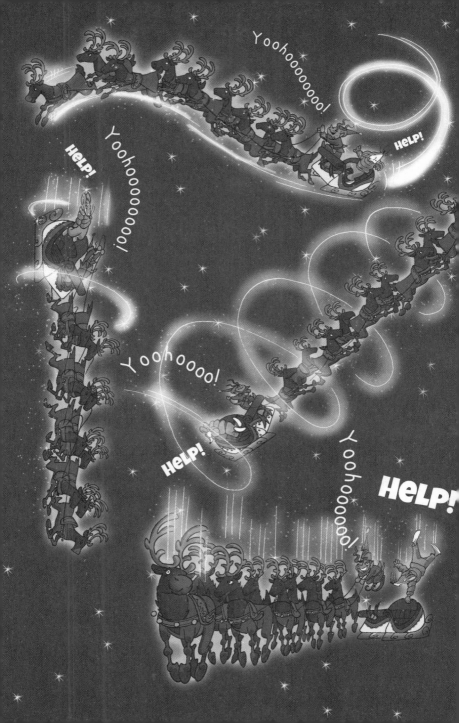

My stomach dropped. My fur turned the colour of mouldy cheese.

"D-d-d-ing-D-d-d-ong!" I stammered. *"I think I'm g-g-g-oing to b-b-be sick!"*

The elf didn't answer. He was too busy guiding the reindeer to do somersaults in the sky. **"YAHOO!"** he yelled, picking up speed. What was that old saying? 'Never talk to a strange elf'? Especially an elf with a name like Ding-Dong.

I was still scolding myself when I noticed the air had suddenly grown colder. It was downright whisker-freezing!

I opened my eyes. What a *magical* sight. Snow and icicle-covered trees glistened like jewels in the moonlight.

We had reached the North Pole.

1. Santa's Workshop
2. Order Department
3. Creative Lab
4. Santa's Office
5. Sled-loading Dock
6. Reindeer Barn
7. Sled Parking Spot
8. Sled Landing Strip
9. Santa's House
10. Elves' Village
11. Gift-packaging Centre
12. Gift Warehouse
13. Post Office
14. Complaint Department

OF COURSE I'M SANTA CLAUS!

Seconds later, Ding-Dong pulled the sleigh to a **SCREECHING HALT** in front of a log cabin.

"This is it, Magazine Mouse. This is where Santa lives," the elf said. He walked up to the door and rang the bell. "It's me, Ding-Dong!" he announced. "I've brought the magazine mouse!"

I coughed. "Well, ahem, actually, sir, I run a newspaper. My name is Stilton, *Geronimo Stilton*," I corrected him.

A booming voice rang out from inside. "Of course. Come on in, dear Geronimo, I've been waiting for you!" it said.

I entered hesitantly. A man with a big round belly and a FLUFFY WHITE BEARD sat in a comfy armchair. He wore a long, fuzzy red robe and slippers with the initials S.C.

"Would you be, I mean, that is, are you him? Are you Santa Claus?" I asked, surprised.

When he laughed, his belly shook like a bowlful of jelly. "Ho, ho, ho! Of course I'm Santa Claus!" he said in a deep, booming voice. **"Who did you think I was? The Easter Bunny?"**

A Bit of a Pickle

Just then, a woman's voice called out sternly, "OK, that's enough now! Go back to sleep, or you'll never get well!"

A minute later, a chubby woman with white hair and sky-blue eyes marched into the room. Can you guess who she was? Yep — Mrs. Claus, Santa's wife.

When she saw me, she stopped and stared.

I smiled. "Mrs. Claus, my name is Stilton, **GERONIMO STILTON**," I said.

Suddenly, she broke into a wide grin. "Oh, Geronimo." She beamed. "We've been waiting for you. Please sit down. Can I get you anything? Hot chocolate? Biscuits? A Cheddar cheese log?" She disappeared into the kitchen.

I turned my attention to

Mrs. Claus, Santa's Wife

Santa. "But, Santa, why? Why did you bring me here?" I squeaked.

Santa sighed. "Well, Geronimo, I seem to be in a little bit of a pickle. I won't be able to deliver the Christmas toys this year," he said.

I gasped. What? That was impossible! I looked closely at Santa. Were his legs broken? Was he having a bad hair day? That's when I noticed his face. It was covered with tiny red spots!

"YIKES!" I cried.

Santa nodded. "I see you've noticed my little problem," he said. "Yes, Geronimo, I've come down with the measles right on my busiest night of the year!"

This was awful. Santa and the elves had worked all year making toys for children. And now they wouldn't be able to deliver them.

Santa with the measles

A tear fell from Santa's eye and landed in his FLUFFY WHITE BEARD. "This is why I need your help, Geronimo. I cannot break my promise to the children. Will you deliver the toys?" he asked.

Me? Deliver toys? I had trouble scampering and chewing gum at the same time.

"Why me, Santa?" I squeaked.

He smiled. "Because I have read every one of your books, dear Geronimo, and you have been on so many **crazy adventures**. This one will be a piece of cake!" he explained.

I was a nervous wreck. How could I, a newspaper mouse, take over Santa's job? It was such an **enormouse** responsibility.

"But what if I mess up? What if the reindeer make fun of me?" I squeaked.

Mrs. Claus put her arm around me. "Of course you can do it,

Geronimo. You just have to believe in yourself," she said.

For some reason, that made me feel a little better. Maybe delivering the toys wouldn't be so hard after all. "I'll do it!" I decided.

Santa and Mrs. Claus beamed. Then Santa wrote something on a piece of paper. He rolled it up, and handed it to me. Then he closed his eyes and went right to sleep.

"ZZZzzzz . . . Finally I can . . . zzzzzzz . . . rest . . . zzzzz!" he snored.

What About Me?!

On my way out, Ding-Dong came running up to me. "So, Mousey, what did Santa tell you?" he asked.

I sighed. "Santa has the measles. He asked me to help him distribute all the toys to children around the world," I said.

The elf turned blue, then purple, then green with envy. **"WHAT?!"** he shrieked. "He asked **YOU**, a mouse, to help him? I don't believe it!"

To prove my point, I unrolled the paper.

It said:

> 'I, Santa Claus, do hereby ask Mr. Geronimo Stilton to manage the workshop while I am ill and to deliver the Christmas toys to children around the world.
> Santa Claus

When Ding-Dong finished reading, he looked like he was about to explode. "**THIS IS SO UNFAIR!** Why did he ask you to help him? What about me?!" he fumed. "This is all because I got a few speeding tickets. What's the big deal?"

I decided not to mention that doing somersaults with the sleigh probably didn't help, either. I felt sort of sorry for the little elf.

"Well, I guess you need to know how to get to Santa's workshop," he grumbled. "Follow me. I'll probably have to tell you how everything works, too."

I nodded. "Ahem, well, yes, thank you. To be honest, I don't know anything about making toys at all," I confessed.

Ding-Dong rolled his eyes. "I kind of guessed it. Imagine a magazine mouse running Santa's toy factory! **WHAT DO YOU KNOW ABOUT TOYS?** All you know about is your silly little magazine!" he complained.

I wanted to point out that The Rodent's Gazette was a newspaper, but I figured that now wasn't the time. Ding-Dong was already in a jealous rage. There was no telling what he might do next! Throw a fit. Throw a tantrum. Throw a LARGE, SKULL-CRUSHING STONE. Instead, I followed him quietly into a huge log warehouse.

That is, I tried to follow him, but he slammed the door on my snout. "Youch!" I screamed.

He snickered. "Oops, sorry, Mousey."

I practised my deep yoga breathing. *Stay calm,* I told myself. *No use getting worked up over a jealous elf.* **Still, I had to admit, Ding-Dong was really starting to get under my fur.**

INSIDE SANTA'S WORKSHOP

Massaging my snout, I stumbled into Santa's workshop. *What an amazing place!* The sound of whirring and buzzing machines filled the air. Elves bustled about here and there, making dolls and baby blocks, toy trains and tracks, baseball bats and balls, and soft, cuddly teddy bears. Some tapped away at **computer keyboards**, programming the latest video games.

Others were busy painting smiling faces on dolls in all different sizes, shapes, and colours.

There were so many things to look at I didn't

know what to check out first. Then I noticed a small printing press. It was churning out a stack of children's books. *How perfect!* I mean, what better gift is there than a book?

Just then, an elf working the printing press noticed me. "Hey, everybody, it's **GERONIMO STILTON**! He's come to help Santa!" he shouted.

"Three cheers for Geronimo Stilton!" another elf added. The room erupted in cheers.

I felt so welcomed. I felt so honoured. **I felt so much pain.** I looked down.

Ding-Dong had just dropped a heavy wooden box right on my paw. I let out a yelp. **"CHEESE NIBLETS!"**

64

"Oops, so sorry, Mousey." Ding-Dong smirked.

Stay calm, I told myself as I gnashed my teeth.

STOP THE CLOCK

The elves helped me load all of the gifts onto the sleigh. Then one of them handed me a looong list of names and addresses. I was just glancing over them when Ding-Dong backed the sleigh up, right over my tail.

"Yikes!" I cried.

The elf giggled under his breath. "Oops, so sorry, Mousey," he murmured.

YIKES!

Stay calm, I told myself as I twisted my throbbing tail up in knots.

The sleigh was packed. The reindeer were in place. Everything was ready. There was just one thing I had to ask before I left.

"How am I ever going to deliver all of these gifts in just one night? There are millions of kids all over the world!" I cried, worried. I pictured the headlines the day after Christmas: SANTA IS A NO-SHOW IN GREECE! NO TOYS FOR TOTS IN NORTH AMERICA!

But Mrs. Claus just smiled. "Don't worry, Geronimo," she said. "Tonight is a magical night. Time will stop only for you. That way, you will be able to give out all of the gifts."

Cheesecake! I was impressed. If I could make time stop, I'd get all of my work done on time. I'd make it to Benjamin's plays. Maybe I'd even be the first mouse in line at CHEESY DOUGHNUTS on Sunday mornings.

I was still thinking about cheesy doughnuts as I waved goodbye to Santa and Mrs. Claus.

"Have a nice trip, Geronimo!" the elves called. Well, except for Ding-Dong. I'm pretty sure he stuck his tongue out at me.

Two minutes later, we took off into the sky. The reindeer **SOARED** through the clouds. A sense of peace and calm fell over me. The reindeer knew exactly where to go. We stopped in every city, large and small. We stopped on islands and in tiny villages. It was an amazing ride! As I dropped off the gifts in each place, I pictured the faces of the happy children opening them the next day.

Christmas truly was a magical holiday!

NOT JUST ANY OLD ELF

Finally, I delivered the last gift. It was for a little girl named Zoe in a small village in Africa. I wished I could stay and learn more about the people who lived there. But I had to get the sleigh back to the North Pole. And besides, how would

I explain why a mouse was dressed up in a Santa suit?

The reindeer headed back to Santa's workshop. I was glad. My tummy had been rumbling for a while now. I couldn't wait for one of Mrs. Claus's delicious Cheddar logs.

As we drew closer to the toy factory, I noticed an elf in the middle of the snow. And not just any old elf. It was Ding-Dong. He was sitting all alone by a **FROZEN LAKE**, staring into the night.

"Hey, Ding-Dong!" I called. "Hop in. I'll give you a ride back to the village."

The elf looked up at me and rolled his eyes. "Well, if it isn't Mr. Big Shot Magazine Mouse," he snorted. "Don't you have more presents to deliver?" He stormed out onto the frozen lake and started twirling around. **"Look at me!"** he yelled. **"I'm Santa Mouse. Squeak! Squeak!"**

Suddenly, there was loud **CRACK!** I stared in horror as the ice split open.

"Watch out!" I squeaked. It was too late.

Within seconds, Ding-Dong had vanished beneath

the icy waters of the frozen lake.

Without thinking, I scampered out after him. My paws made the ice creak noisily beneath me. I was a nervous wreck. **What if I couldn't save Ding-Dong?**

I lay down on the ice and slid towards the elf. I could just make out his tiny hand waving desperately in the air.

"Help!" he cried in a shaky voice.

Quickly, I took off my belt and threw it towards him. "Grab the other end!"

Ding-Dong grabbed the belt. Very slowly, I managed to pull him out of the **FREEZING WATER**. I wrapped him up in my warm red jacket. Then I brought him back to the village.

Santa and Mrs. Claus were shocked to see what had happened to Ding-Dong. Mrs. Claus made him lie on the sofa. She gave him a cup of warm milk with lots of honey.

After he warmed up, Ding-Dong threw me a shy smile. "Guess you're not such a bad mouse after all, Geronimo," he said. Then he jumped up and shook my paw.

I grinned. Ding-Dong wasn't big on words. **But I knew he was grateful that I had saved his life.**

CHEDDAR LOGS FOR EVERYONE

I was feeling warm and happy. What a night! I sat by the fire with Santa and Mrs. Claus, chatting away, munching on treats, and drinking cups of hot chocolate. Mrs. Claus's Cheddar logs really are OUT OF THIS WORLD!

"How can I ever thank you for all that you have done, Geronimo?" Santa asked.

I shook my head. "Mmmfl, mmmmfll," I mumbled, my mouth full of cheese.

"Ho! Ho! Ho!" He chuckled. "I thought you might not ask for anything in return. You're a *real gentlemouse*, Geronimo Stilton." He laughed. "But I want to give you a gift anyway."

I wondered what Santa would give me. A new suit? A tie? A box of chocolate Cheesy Chews? My mouth began to water just thinking about it.

But instead of a wrapped gift, Santa pulled out a stack of letters. He explained that the letters were from children all over the world. "Every year, I get letters from children asking for dolls and teddy bears, race cars and bicycles. But once in a while, I get a letter from a child asking for **something I cannot make**," he said. "It makes me very sad. But this year, I think you can help me with one of those letters, Geronimo."

He flipped through the envelopes and handed me a

tiny sheet of paper. I couldn't believe my eyes. It was a letter from my favourite nephew, Benjamin:

dear Santa Claus,
this year, i'm not going to ask you for presents. what i really want most in the world is for my uncle geronimo to spend more time with me.
    he's always so busy that i hardly ever get to see him.
    i'm sorry about that, because i love him very much.
    thanks, Santa.
    your friend,
    benjamin Stilton

My heart dropped. "But I love my nephew with all my heart!" I protested. "I always make time for him."

Just then, Santa pulled out a tiny black book. "According to my notes, Geronimo, the last time you played with your nephew Benjamin was exactly **ONE MONTH AND TWELVE DAYS AGO**," he said quietly.

Yikes! How embarrassing. How mortifying. How true! My fur turned beet red. I hadn't been spending much time at all with Benjamin lately. I was so busy with work I had forgotten him.

"The real spirit of Christmas isn't just about spending money on gifts, dear Geronimo," Santa said. "It's about spending time with the ones we love."

I nodded. Santa was right. Even though it made me sad, I was glad he had shown me Benjamin's letter. I would never want to hurt my nephew. I couldn't wait to get back to Mouse Island to see him. But first, I decided to take a quick snooze. **After all, travelling around the world in one night can really take a lot out of a mouse.**

THE MOST IMPORTANT THING

I was happily snoring away when a loud knock woke me up. Was it Santa?

I blinked and looked around. What was happening? I was sitting behind my desk at The Rodent's Gazette.

Sun streamed through the window. It was morning. How very strange. Had I been sleeping? Was my adventure with Santa all just a dream?

I was still trying to make sense of everything when I heard another loud knock at my door. Two seconds later, Grandfather William burst into the office.

CHEESE NIBLETS, here it comes, I thought. Grandfather's going to pull out my whiskers now that he's caught me **SLEEPING** on the job. But instead of squeaking about my sleeping on the job, Grandfather William began squeaking about something else.

"Grandson! What are you still doing in the office?" he thundered. "We waited for you all last night. It's Christmas! You need to be with the rodents you love!"

I was so confused. "But, Grandfather, you kept telling me that I needed

to work, work, work. You said you would take over my job if I didn't," I stammered.

Grandfather William chuckled. "Oh, Grandson, you're so **GULLIBLE**! Don't you know a joke when you hear one?" he squeaked. "Work is important. But your family is the *most important thing in the world*!"

With that, Grandfather William turned and left the office. Right then, I remembered something. I had never written my article on the true spirit of Christmas.

I wracked my brain for ideas. But I couldn't think of a thing. Not one sentence. Not one word. I was a big blank.

What could I do?

Ways to Get an Idea

1. TAKE A HOT BATH WITH LOTS AND LOTS OF CHEDDAR BUBBLES.

2. DO A LITTLE YOGA.

3. WRITE WITH A FAVOURITE PEN OR PENCIL.

4. LISTEN TO CLASSICAL MUSIC.

5. STAND ON YOUR HEAD.

6. CUT LITTLE STARS OUT OF MODELLING CLAY.

7. PUT AWAY YOUR LAUNDRY.

ONE MORE CHEESE LOG

Right then, I remembered something my aunt Sweetfur used to tell me when I was a **young mouse**. Just before I left for school she'd say, "The brain cannot function if the body is not well fed. Always eat a good breakfast and you'll be able to concentrate better."

I fixed myself a nice cup of hot chocolate and a fresh cheese log. As I sat nibbling on the yummy cheese log, I thought about my visit with Santa and Mrs. Claus. **Oh, what a wonderful dream!**

An idea popped into my head. That was it! I could write about my amazing dream.

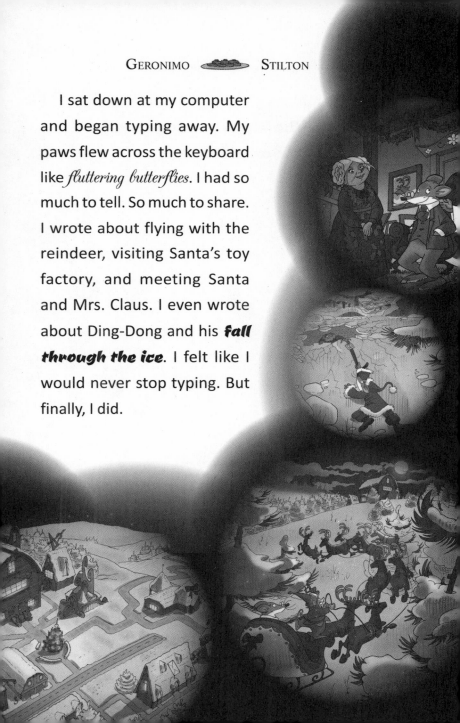

I sat down at my computer and began typing away. My paws flew across the keyboard like *fluttering butterflies*. I had so much to tell. So much to share. I wrote about flying with the reindeer, visiting Santa's toy factory, and meeting Santa and Mrs. Claus. I even wrote about Ding-Dong and his **fall through the ice**. I felt like I would never stop typing. But finally, I did.

I leaned back in my chair and sighed happily. **Who knew you could learn so much from a dream?**

I'M SORRY!

Before I left the office, I decided to make a few phone calls. Well, maybe more than a few. In fact, I guess you could say I called everyone. All of my friends, my relatives, my co-workers.

I needed to tell everyone I was sorry for ignoring them. I invited them all to my house. "We'll have a great big Christmas party," I said. "Bring your friends, bring your family. We'll all celebrate together! After all, that's what the true Christmas spirit is all about!"

Everyone accepted the invitation. I was so **EXCITED**. I was finally getting into the

Christmas spirit. I couldn't wait to celebrate with my friends and family. I grabbed my coat and ran home as fast as my paws would carry me.

But when I got there, I realised I had forgotten a few things. I didn't have any food in my fridge. I didn't have any Christmas decorations hung up. I didn't even have a single present.

PUTRID CHEESE PUFFS! What was I thinking? I would never be able to get everything together in such a short time!

But just as I was about to pull out all of my fur, the doorbell rang.

DING DONG DING DONG
DING DONG DING DONG

WE CAME TO HELP YOU, GERONIMO!

I raced to my front door and yanked it open. A huge crowd stood on my doorstep. I tried to shoo them away. I didn't have time for visitors. I didn't have time for carol-singers. I didn't have time for salesmice. I had very dear friends and family coming over!

"It's Christmas," I squeaked. "Don't you rodents have somewhere to go?"

The mice laughed. "We came to help you set up for the party, Geronimo!" they shouted.

I blinked. **OOPS.** When would I ever learn to stop putting my paw in my mouth? Standing right in front of me were my very dear friends and family!

In a flash, my house was bustling.

Some mice decorated the Christmas tree.

Some started a **FIRE** in the fireplace.

Others set the table.

And my good friend Saucy Le Paws whipped up a *super-fabumouse* cheesy lasagne. Do you know Saucy? He's one of the most famous chefs on Mouse Island.

It was truly a wonderful party. In fact, I think I could honestly say it was the best Christmas I've ever had. Cross my paws over my heart!

It felt good to have my friends and family around. I had been so busy with work at the office that I had forgotten how much I enjoyed just hanging out and squeaking with the ones I loved.

I raised my glass and made a toast.

"Thank you all for coming today. I hope you all know how much I value your friendship, and I'm sorry if I've been ignoring you lately. I let my work take over, and I promise to never let that happen again. **I love you all too much!**" I said.

Everyone clapped and hugged me. Well, everyone except my obnoxious cousin Trap. He was too busy stuffing his snout with lasagne. **That mouse would eat me out of house and hole if I let him.**

92

MERRY CHRISTMAS

Snow, Snow, and More Snow!

We were so busy celebrating, no one noticed the snow piling up outside. When I finally looked out of the window, the snow was five feet high. And it was still coming down!

"HOLEY CHEESE!" I squeaked. "We've never had this kind of a blizzard in New Mouse City before!"

I turned on the TV. We all huddled around it to hear the news.

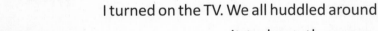

The entire city was **BURIED** under snow! The sick and the elderly could not get around because the snow blocked the streets.

New Mouse City's mayor, the Honourable Frederick Fuzzypaws, appeared on the screen.

"Citizens of New Mouse City, we have a big problem!" he announced. "The city is paralysed by snow. Ambulances cannot get to sick rodents. Fire engines cannot get to fires. Cheese delivery trucks cannot get to the Stop and Squeak."

Next to me, my cousin looked faint. **"No cheese?"** he gasped in horror.

On the screen, the mayor continued. "There is only one way to fix this problem. I ask that every mouse pick up a shovel. **Together, we can help New Mouse City!**"

I turned off the TV. Everyone looked at one another. It was so warm and cosy inside my mouse hole. And it was so cold outside. But our city needed us. We armed ourselves with shovels and headed outside.

We shovelled pavements and driveways. We shovelled

front steps and back steps. We even shovelled the whole town square. I was so tired I thought my paws would fall off. **Did I mention I'm not much of a muscle mouse?** Still, I kept on shovelling. By nightfall, the streets of New Mouse City were finally cleared.

We celebrated by drinking cups of steaming hot chocolate. I was exhausted, but I was happy. I hugged my nephew Benjamin. I had no gift to give him this year – except for the gift of myself.

"From now on, I will not let work get in the way of our relationship," I told him. "I will always make time for my **favourite nephew**."

Benjamin's eyes lit up. I smiled. Outside, a cold December wind rattled the windows. But inside, I felt warm and peaceful.

Oh, what a strange and wonderful Christmas it had been. I'd learned so much from my dream about the North Pole. I thought about Santa and Mrs. Claus. I thought about the elves and the reindeer. I even thought about Ding-Dong, my new elf friend. It all seemed so real!

I stared out the window thinking about everything.
And for a minute I thought I could almost hear a tiny
voice in the distance calling,

"Merry Christmas to all, and to all a good night!"

Lots of Ideas for a Special Christmas!

Sparkling Pine Cones

What you need: pine cones, soft brush, gold or silver paint, paintbrush, glitter, yarn

1. Gather pine cones that have fallen from the trees and dust them lightly with a soft brush.

2. Paint each pine cone with either the gold or silver paint.

3. While the paint is still wet, sprinkle glitter on top to make the pine cones sparkle.

4. Wrap the yarn around the base of each pine cone. Tie the two ends of the yarn together to make a loop.

5. Hang the pine cone as a decoration on your Christmas tree!

Scented Half-Moons

What you need: three oranges, knife, cutting
board, red or green ribbon

1. Ask an adult to slice the oranges in half, and then in half again on a cutting board, so that you have the shape of a half-moon. Let them dry someplace warm for five days.

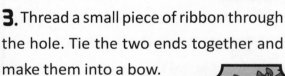

2. When the oranges are completely dry, ask an adult to poke a hole through the top of each slice.

3. Thread a small piece of ribbon through the hole. Tie the two ends together and make them into a bow.

4. Hang this decoration on your Christmas tree. It will give the whole room a wonderful scent.

Colourful Decorations

What you need: polystyrene balls, ice lolly sticks, glue, different-coloured dried seeds (green lentils, red beans, corn, and sunflower seeds), varnish, brushes, red ribbon

1. Push an ice lolly stick into a polystyrene ball. Brush a thin layer of glue onto the ball. Take a handful of the same kind of coloured seeds and glue them onto the ball. Be sure to place them very close to one another. Let them dry well.

2. Spread varnish over the seeded ball with a brush.

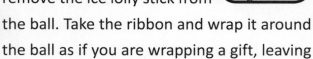

3. Once the varnish is dry, remove the ice lolly stick from the ball. Take the ribbon and wrap it around the ball as if you are wrapping a gift, leaving a few inches of ribbon on either end. Tie these into a bow to hang on the Christmas tree.

4. Repeat the steps above with the rest of the balls, using all the different types of seeds.

Brightly Shining Stars

What you need: round cookie cutter, pencil, yellow paper, safety scissors, star cookie cutter, glue stick, transparent paper, glitter, red ribbon

1. Take the round cookie cutter and, with the pencil, trace around it on yellow paper. Cut out the shape with safety scissors.

2. Using the other cookie cutter, trace a star in the centre of the yellow circle.

3. Cut out the star with the safety scissors. The circle should now have a star-shaped hole in its centre.

4. Use a glue stick to apply the transparent paper behind the circle and cut out the excess paper around it. On the right side, carefully apply glue on the transparent paper, and sprinkle glitter over the hollow star.

5. Ask an adult to make a hole at the top of the decoration. Thread a red ribbon through the hole, make a loop, and hang it on your Christmas tree.

THE RODENT'S GAZETTE

1. Main entrance
2. Printing presses (where everything is printed)
3. Accounts department
4. Editorial room (where editors, illustrators, and designers work)
5. Geronimo Stilton's office
6. Geronimo's botanical garden

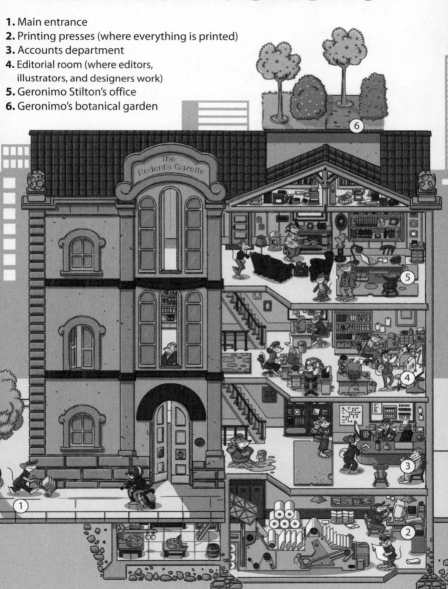

MAP OF NEW MOUSE CITY

1. Industrial Zone
2. Cheese Factories
3. Angorat International Airport
4. WRAT Radio and Television Station
5. Cheese Market
6. Fish Market
7. Town Hall
8. Snotnose Castle
9. The Seven Hills of Mouse Island
10. Mouse Central Station
11. Trade Centre
12. Movie Theatre
13. Gym
14. Catnegie Hall
15. Singing Stone Plaza
16. The Gouda Theatre
17. Grand Hotel
18. Mouse General Hospital
19. Botanical Gardens
20. Cheap Junk for Less (Trap's store)
21. Parking Lot
22. Museum of Modern Art
23. University and Library
24. The Daily Rat
25. The Rodent's Gazette
26. Trap's House
27. Fashion District
28. The Mouse House Restaurant
29. Environmental Protection Centre
30. Harbour Office
31. Mousidon Square Garden
32. Golf Course
33. Swimming Pool
34. Blushing Meadow Tennis Courts
35. Curlyfur Island Amusement Park
36. Geronimo's House
37. Historic District
38. Public Library
39. Shipyard
40. Thea's House
41. New Mouse Harbour
42. Luna Lighthouse
43. The Statue of Liberty
44. Hercule Poirat's Office
45. Petunia Pretty Paws's House
46. Grandfather William's House

MAP OF MOUSE ISLAND

1. Big Ice Lake
2. Frozen Fur Peak
3. Slipperyslopes Glacier
4. Coldcreeps Peak
5. Ratzikistan
6. Transratania
7. Mount Vamp
8. Roastedrat Volcano
9. Brimstone Lake
10. Poopedcat Pass
11. Stinko Peak
12. Dark Forest
13. Vain Vampires Valley
14. Goosebumps Gorge
15. The Shadow Line Pass
16. Penny-Pincher Castle
17. Nature Reserve Park
18. Las Ratayas Marinas
19. Fossil Forest
20. Lake Lake
21. Lake Lakelake
22. Lake Lakelakelake
23. Cheddar Crag
24. Cannycat Castle
25. Valley of the Giant Sequoia
26. Cheddar Springs
27. Sulphurous Swamp
28. Old Reliable Geyser
29. Vole Vale
30. Ravingrat Ravine
31. Gnat Marshes
32. Munster Highlands
33. Mousehara Desert
34. Oasis of the Sweaty Camel
35. Cabbagehead Hill
36. Rattytrap Jungle
37. Rio Mosquito
38. Mousefort Beach
39. San Mouscisco
40. Swissville
41. Cheddarton
42. Mouseport
43. New Mouse City
44. Pirate Ship of Cats

THE COLLECTION

HAVE YOU READ ALL OF GERONIMO'S ADVENTURES?

ABOUT THE AUTHOR

Born in New Mouse City, Mouse Island, GERONIMO STILTON is Rattus Emeritus of Mousomorphic Literature and of Neo-Ratonic Comparative Philosophy. For the past twenty years, he has been running The Rodent's Gazette, New Mouse City's most widely read daily newspaper.

Stilton was awarded the Ratitzer Prize for his scoops on *The Curse of the Cheese Pyramid* and *The Search for Sunken Treasure*. He has also received the Andersen Prize for Personality of the Year. His works have been published all over the globe.

In his spare time, Mr. Stilton collects antique cheese rinds and plays golf. But what he most enjoys is telling stories to his nephew Benjamin.